Even more than
a sloth loves
to sleep.

I love you
more than a
cricket loves
to chirp.

Even more than a fly
loves to slurp.

It isn't a lie.
I love you more than
a bird loves to fly.

I love you more
than an owl
loves to hoot.

Even more than a racoon loves to loot.

I love you more than
a panther loves to growl.

Even more than a
wolf loves to howl.

I love you more than a dog loves to fetch.

Even more than a giraffe loves to stretch.

I love you more than a peacock loves to model.

Even more than a penguin loves to waddle.

I love you more than a hummingbird loves to flap.

Even more than a crocodile
loves to snap.

You can see it is true.
I love you more than
a panda loves bamboo.

Even more than
a sloth loves
to sleep.

I love you
more than a
cricket loves
to chirp.

Even more than a fly
loves to slurp.

It isn't a lie.
I love you more than
a bird loves to fly.

I love you more
than an owl
loves to hoot.

Even more than a
racoon loves to loot.

COOKIES

I love you more than
a panther loves to growl.

Even more than a
wolf loves to howl.

I love you more than a
dog loves to fetch.

Even more than
a giraffe loves
to stretch.

I love you more than a peacock loves to model.

Even more than a penguin loves to waddle.

I love you more than a hummingbird loves to flap.

Even more than a crocodile loves to snap.

You can see it is true.
I love you more than
a panda loves bamboo.